Frederick

Frederick

Leo Lionni

 Alfred A. Knopf, New York

www.randomhouse.com / kids

Library of Congress Cataloging-in-Publication Data
Lionni, Leo.
Frederick / by Leo Lionni.
p.   cm.
Summary: Frederick the field mouse sat on the old stone wall while his four brothers gathered food for the approaching winter days. The other mice felt that Frederick was not doing his share of the work, but when the food ran out, Frederick saved the day with what he had gathered.
ISBN 0-394-81040-6 (trade) — ISBN 0-394-91040-0 (lib. bdg.)
[1. Mice—Stories. 2. Picture books for children.]
I. Title.
66-10355

Printed in Mexico   36   35   34   33   32   31

Frederick

All along the meadow where the cows grazed and the horses ran, there was an old stone wall.

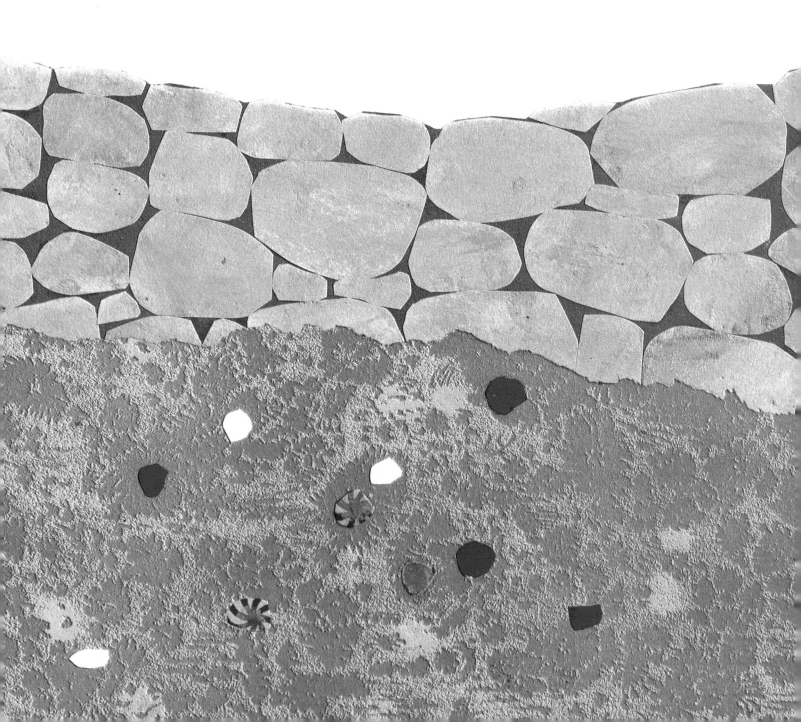

In that wall, not far from the barn and the granary,
a chatty family of field mice had their home.

But the farmers had moved away, the barn was abandoned, and the granary stood empty. And since winter was not far off, the little mice began to gather corn and nuts and wheat and straw. They all worked day and night.
All — except Frederick.

"Frederick, why don't you work?" they asked.
"I *do* work," said Frederick.
"I gather sun rays for the cold dark winter days."

And when they saw Frederick sitting there, staring at the meadow, they said, "And now, Frederick?" "I gather colors," answered Frederick simply. "For winter is gray."

And once Frederick seemed half asleep. "Are you dreaming, Frederick?" they asked reproachfully. But Frederick said, "Oh no, I am gathering words. For the winter days are long and many, and we'll run out of things to say."

The winter days came, and when the first snow fell
the five little field mice took to their hideout in the stones.

In the beginning there was lots to eat,
and the mice told stories of foolish foxes
and silly cats. They were a happy family.

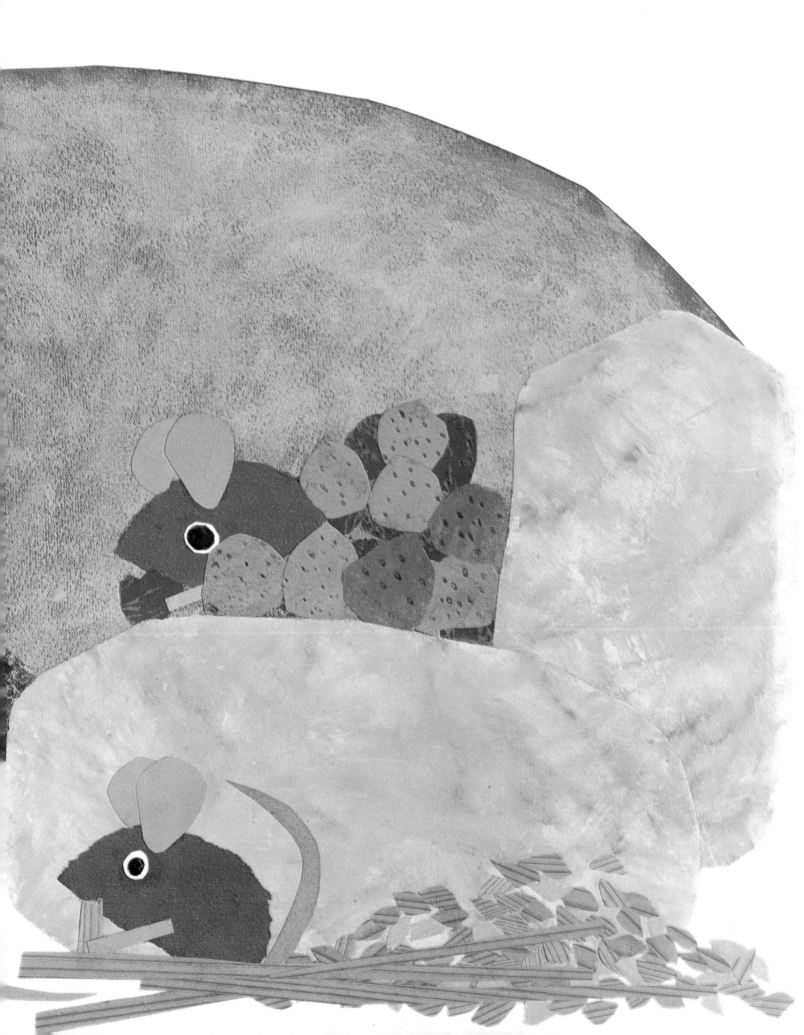

But little by little they had nibbled up
most of the nuts and berries, the straw was
gone, and the corn was only a memory.
It was cold in the wall
and no one felt like chatting.

Then they remembered
what Frederick had said about sun rays
and colors and words.
"What about *your* supplies, Frederick?"
they asked.

"Close your eyes," said Frederick,
as he climbed on a big stone.
"Now I send you the rays of the sun.
Do you feel how their golden glow ... "
And as Frederick spoke of the sun
the four little mice
began to feel warmer.
Was it Frederick's voice?
Was it magic?

"And how about the colors, Frederick?"
they asked anxiously. "Close your eyes again,"
Frederick said. And when he told them
of the blue periwinkles,
the red poppies in the yellow wheat,
and the green leaves
of the berry bush,
they saw the colors as clearly
as if they had been painted
in their minds.

"And the words, Frederick?"

Frederick cleared his throat,
waited a moment, and then,
as if from a stage, he said:

When Frederick had finished

"Who scatters snowflakes? Who melts the ice?
Who spoils the weather? Who makes it nice?
Who grows the four-leaf clovers in June?
Who dims the daylight? Who lights the moon?

Four little field mice who live in the sky.
Four little field mice . . . like you and I.

One is the Springmouse who turns on the showers.
Then comes the Summer who paints in the flowers.
The Fallmouse is next with walnuts and wheat.
And Winter is last . . . with little cold feet.

Aren't we lucky the seasons are four?
Think of a year with one less . . . or one more!"

they all applauded. "But Frederick," they said, "you are a poet!"

Frederick blushed, took a bow, and said shyly, "I know it."

Frederick Frederick